NICK
the fairly
OddParents

PICK A DAD, ANY DAD!

adapted by Steven Banks
illustrated by Harry Moore

based on a teleplay by Andrew Nicholls and Darrell Vickers

Simon Spotlight/Nickelodeon

New York   London   Toronto   Sydney

Butch Hartman

Based on the TV series *The Fairly OddParents*™ created by Butch Hartman as seen on Nickelodeon®

SIMON SPOTLIGHT

An imprint of Simon & Schuster Children's Publishing Division

1230 Avenue of the Americas, New York, New York 10020

Copyright © 2005 Viacom International Inc. All rights reserved. NICKELODEON, *The Fairly OddParents*, and all related titles, logos, and characters are trademarks of Viacom International Inc.

SIMON SPOTLIGHT and colophon are registered trademarks of Simon & Schuster, Inc.

Nelvana is the International Representative. NELVANA® Nelvana Limited. CORUS™ Corus Entertainment Inc.

Manufactured in the United States of America

First Edition

2 4 6 8 10 9 7 5 3 1

ISBN 0-689-87185-6

Timmy Turner was practicing his knot-tying skills for the Squirrely Scout Father and Son Camping Festival.

"This year Dad and I are going to win the Golden Acorn award!" he announced. Cosmo and Wanda, his fairy godparents, watched him get all tangled up in the rope.

"I think you may need help!" said Wanda.

"I can help!" said Cosmo. "I used to be a Fairy Scout! I got an 'almost helped an old lady across the street' merit badge!"

"I hope Timmy is a better Scout than you were," said Wanda.

Timmy smiled. "I don't have to be! My dad was a Flying Squirrel! That's the highest rank of Squirrely Scout there is! I know we'll win!"

Timmy's dad popped his head in the door. "Hi, Timmy! Can't do anything with you right now! Busy working! Bye, Timmy!"

He ran off to the garage.

"I need to find a supercool replacement dad," said Timmy. "And fast!"

"But how can you replace your dad?" asked Wanda.

Just then Timmy's friend A.J. and his dad appeared in robo-walkers.

"These robot suits are awesome!" said A.J. "You're the best dad ever!"

Timmy turned to Cosmo and Wanda. "I wish A.J.'s dad was my dad!" POOF!

Timmy was in A.J.'s bedroom, and A.J.'s dad was *his* dad!

"Hey, new smart Dad!" said Timmy. "I bet you know a ton about camping and would help me win the Golden Acorn!"

"Absolutely, son!" said A.J.'s dad. "I've read every book on the subject, including three I wrote myself!"

"All right!" shouted Timmy. "Let's get out there and get dirty!"

"Why get icky and dirty?" asked A.J.'s dad. "With my Virtual Camper Program you have all the fun of camping without the camping!"

"Or the fun," Timmy said, sighing.

A.J.'s dad put virtual reality glasses on himself and Timmy. "Look!" he shouted. "There's a campfire, and marshmallows, and trees, and bees chasing me! Help!"

"What good is it if we don't really get to go camping?" complained Timmy. "I wish I was back home!" POOF!

"I need to find a dad who isn't afraid to go outside and get dirty," said Timmy.
Just then Timmy saw Chester and his dad flying kites.

"These kites are great!" shouted Chester. "You're the best filthy dad ever!"

"Hmmm. Chester's dad is not afraid to get dirty," said Timmy. "He's perfect! I wish Chester's dad was my dad!" POOF!

"Okay, Timmy, my son," said Chester's dad. "Ready to go camping, and to hunt and trap our own food?"

"You bet!" said Timmy.

The next thing he knew, Timmy was at the Dimmsdale Zoo!

"What do you want to eat?" asked Chester's dad. "Lion? Tiger? Bear? Oh, my!"

"Is this legal?" asked Timmy.

"Don't know, but it sure is easy!" said Chester's dad.

Timmy turned to Cosmo and Wanda. "Help!"

POOF!

"Maybe I should ask my dad again?" Timmy wondered aloud. "Maybe he's not so busy anymore."

Timmy knocked on the garage door. "Dad?"

His dad poked his head out. "Sorry, son! Too busy to talk, think, or even breathe!"

"I'm running out of dads!" said Timmy.

Suddenly Sanjay and his stepdad came jogging down the street. Sanjay was chanting as he ran:

"I don't know, but I've been told, my stepdad's . . . as good as gold!"

Timmy's eyes lit up. "A *step*dad! Sanjay's stepdad is a marine who's not afraid of anything! He's tough as nails! I wish he was my dad!" POOF!

"Rise and shine, soldier," shouted Sanjay's stepdad. "It's five a.m.! Drop and give me fifty, mister!"

Timmy started doing push-ups. "Can we go to the camping festival?"

"Yes, we can!" said Sanjay's stepdad. "But first we'll run a hundred miles, do five hundred jumping jacks, and swim ten miles!"

Timmy looked down at Cosmo and Wanda. "I wish I was out of here!" POOF!

"I give up," said Timmy. "I'll never find a replacement for my dad!"

"What did you say?" asked Cosmo. "Your dad is making so much noise in the garage that I couldn't hear you!"

"I quit!" shouted Timmy. "The campout starts in ten minutes! I'll never make it!"

"Why don't you go and see what your father's doing?" Wanda suggested.

Timmy went inside the garage and couldn't believe his eyes!

"Dad!" shouted Timmy. "What is that?"

"It's a solar-powered rocket made out of toothpicks and gum," said
Timmy's dad proudly. "I call it the I'm-So-Proud-to-Be-Timmy's-Dad Rocket!"

"Can we use the rocket to get to the Squirrely Scout Father and Son Camping Festival?" asked Timmy.

"That's why I built it!" replied his dad. Timmy and his dad jumped into the rocket.

"Three, two, one, liftoff!" shouted Timmy.

Timmy and his dad got to the camping festival in ten seconds!

"This is the most amazing thing I've ever seen," said the Squirrely Scout master. "You and your father win the Golden Acorn Award!"

"I'm glad you're my dad, Dad," said Timmy. "I wouldn't want anyone else!"

"Gee, I can't imagine what it would be like to have someone else as your dad," said Timmy's dad.

Timmy grinned. "*I can!*"